MOTHER GOOSE

A Treasury of Best-Loved Rhymes

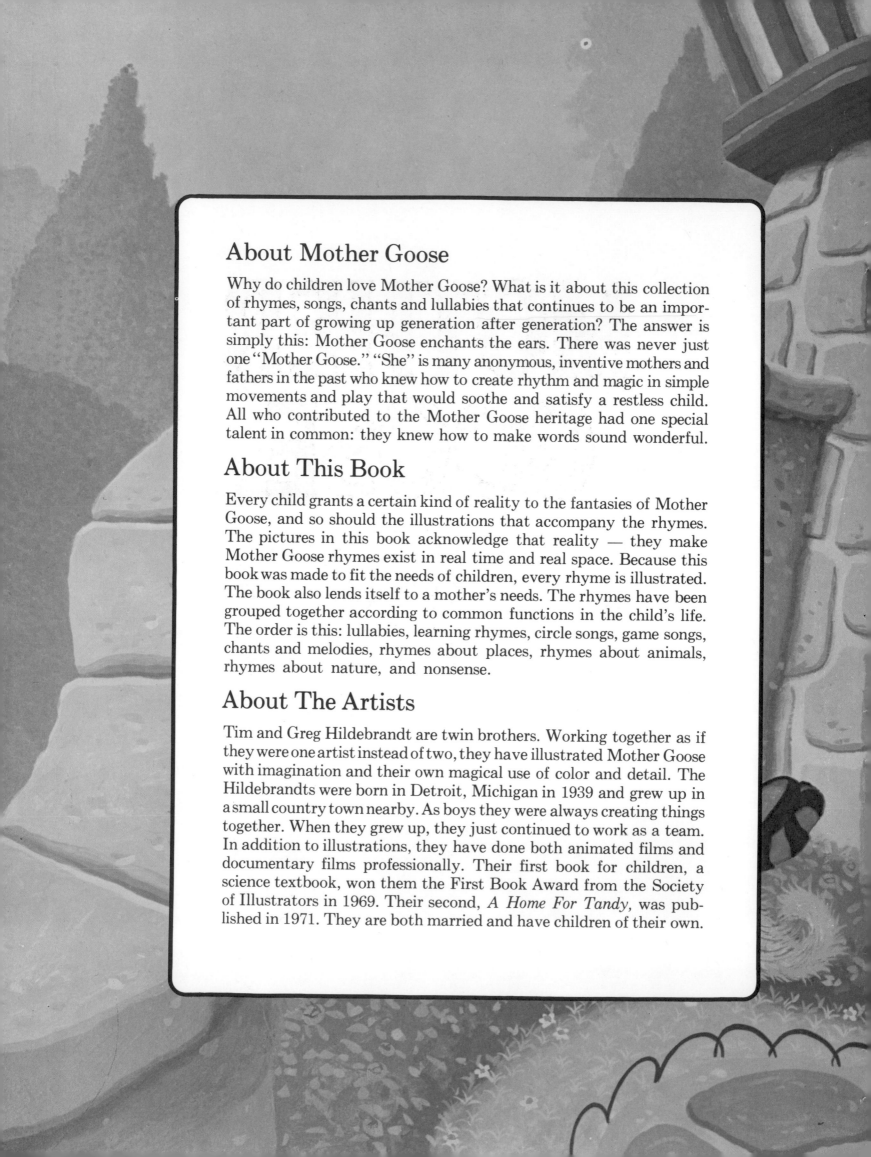

About Mother Goose

Why do children love Mother Goose? What is it about this collection of rhymes, songs, chants and lullabies that continues to be an important part of growing up generation after generation? The answer is simply this: Mother Goose enchants the ears. There was never just one "Mother Goose." "She" is many anonymous, inventive mothers and fathers in the past who knew how to create rhythm and magic in simple movements and play that would soothe and satisfy a restless child. All who contributed to the Mother Goose heritage had one special talent in common: they knew how to make words sound wonderful.

About This Book

Every child grants a certain kind of reality to the fantasies of Mother Goose, and so should the illustrations that accompany the rhymes. The pictures in this book acknowledge that reality — they make Mother Goose rhymes exist in real time and real space. Because this book was made to fit the needs of children, every rhyme is illustrated. The book also lends itself to a mother's needs. The rhymes have been grouped together according to common functions in the child's life. The order is this: lullabies, learning rhymes, circle songs, game songs, chants and melodies, rhymes about places, rhymes about animals, rhymes about nature, and nonsense.

About The Artists

Tim and Greg Hildebrandt are twin brothers. Working together as if they were one artist instead of two, they have illustrated Mother Goose with imagination and their own magical use of color and detail. The Hildebrandts were born in Detroit, Michigan in 1939 and grew up in a small country town nearby. As boys they were always creating things together. When they grew up, they just continued to work as a team. In addition to illustrations, they have done both animated films and documentary films professionally. Their first book for children, a science textbook, won them the First Book Award from the Society of Illustrators in 1969. Their second, *A Home For Tandy,* was published in 1971. They are both married and have children of their own.

MOTHER GOOSE

A Treasury of Best-Loved Rhymes

Edited by Watty Piper

Illustrated by
Tim and Greg Hildebrandt

Platt & Munk, Publishers/New York

A Division of Grosset & Dunlap

CONTENTS

Copyright©1972 by Platt & Munk. All rights reserved.

Printed in the United States of America.

Library of Congress Catalog Card No. 72-185630

ISBN 0-448-47230-9 (Trade Edition)
ISBN 0-448-13027-0 (Library Edition)

OLD MOTHER GOOSE

Old Mother Goose,
When she wanted to wander,
Would ride through the air
On a very fine gander.

Mother Goose had a house,
'Twas built in a wood,
Where an owl at the door
For sentinel stood.

8

HUSH-A-BYE BABY

Hush-a-bye, baby,
On the tree top,
When the wind blows
The cradle will rock.
When the bough bends
The cradle will fall,
And down will come baby,
Cradle and all.

ROCK-A-BYE BABY

Rock-a-bye, baby,
Thy cradle is green,
Father's a nobleman,
Mother's a queen.
Betty's a lady,
And wears a gold ring,
And Johnny's a drummer,
And drums for the king.

SLEEP, BABY, SLEEP

Sleep, baby, sleep,
Thy father guards the sheep,
Thy mother shakes
    the dreamland tree
And from it fall
    sweet dreams for thee,
Sleep, baby, sleep.

HUSH LITTLE BABY

Hush, little baby, don't say a word,
Papa's going to buy you a
    mocking bird.
If the mocking bird won't sing,
Papa's going to buy you a
    diamond ring.
If the diamond ring turns to brass,
Papa's going to buy you a
    looking glass.
If the looking glass gets broke,
Papa's going to buy you a billy goat.
If the billy goat runs away,
Papa's going to buy you another
    today.

HOW MANY DAYS
How many days has my baby
  to play?
Saturday, Sunday, Monday,
Tuesday, Wednesday,
  Thursday, Friday,
Saturday, Sunday, Monday.

ONE, TWO, BUCKLE MY SHOE
One, two, buckle my shoe,
Three, four, shut the door,
Five, six, pick up sticks,
Seven, eight, lay them straight,
Nine, ten, big fat hen.

RIDE AWAY, RIDE AWAY

Ride away, ride away,
Johnny shall ride,
And he shall have Pussy Cat
Tied to one side.
He shall have Puppy Dog
Tied to the other,
And Johnny shall ride
To see his grandmother.

MY LADY'S KNIVES AND FORKS

Here's my lady's knives
    and forks,
Here's my lady's table,
Here's my lady's looking glass,
And here's the baby's cradle.

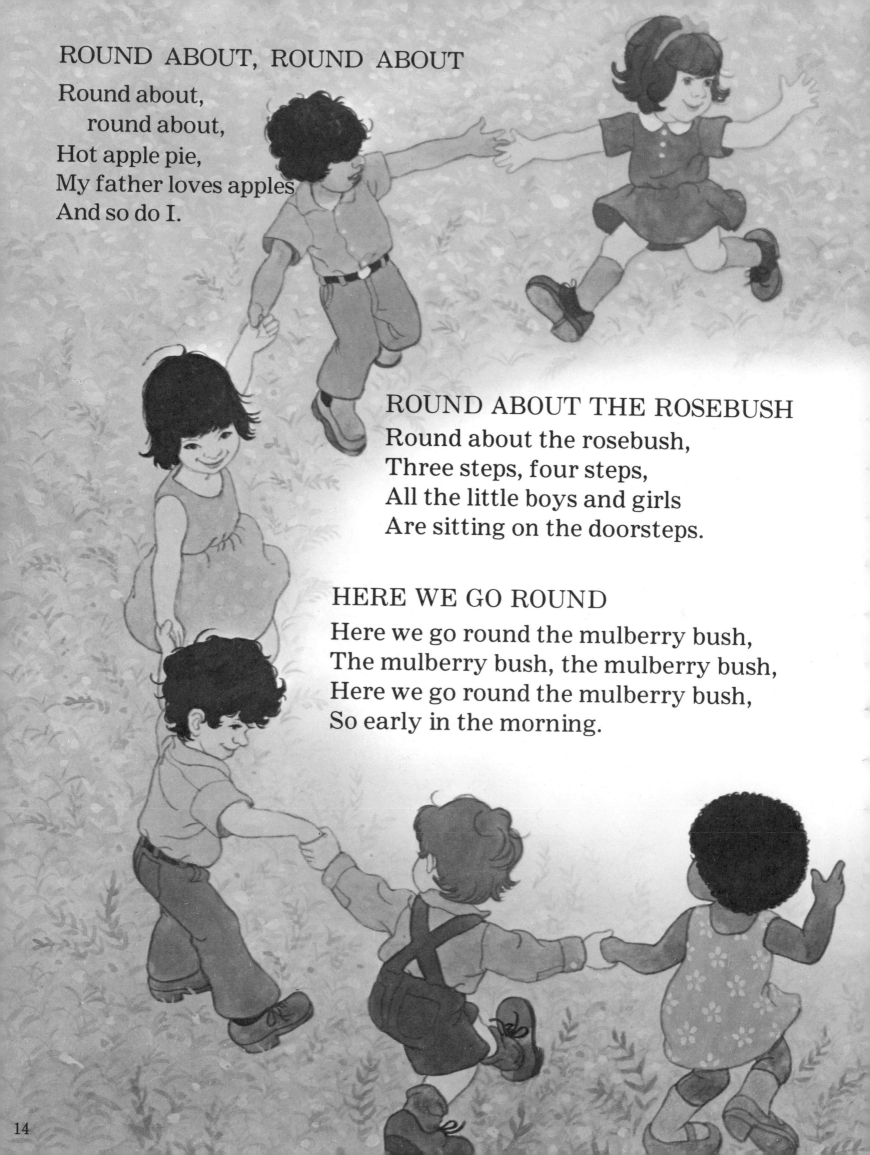

ROUND ABOUT, ROUND ABOUT

Round about,
  round about,
Hot apple pie,
My father loves apples
And so do I.

ROUND ABOUT THE ROSEBUSH

Round about the rosebush,
Three steps, four steps,
All the little boys and girls
Are sitting on the doorsteps.

HERE WE GO ROUND

Here we go round the mulberry bush,
The mulberry bush, the mulberry bush,
Here we go round the mulberry bush,
So early in the morning.

SALLY GO ROUND THE SUN

Sally go round the sun,
Sally go round the moon,
Sally go round the chimney pots
On a Saturday afternoon.

HERE WE GO UP, UP, UP

Here we go up, up, up,
Here we go down, down, down,
Here we go backward and forward,
Here we go round and round.

RING AROUND
THE ROSIES

Ring around the rosies,
A pocket full of posies,
Hush! Hush! Hush!
All fall down.

FLYING KITE, FLYING KITE

Flying kite, flying kite,
Up in the sky,
Where are you going to,
Flying so high?

SEE-SAW, SAC-ARA-DOWN

See-saw, sac-ara-down,
Which is the way
   to London town?
One foot up
   and one foot down,
That's the way
   to London town.

SEE-SAW, MARGERY DAW

See-saw, Margery Daw,
Johnny shall have
   a new master.
He shall have
   but a penny a day
Because he can't work
   any faster.

LONDON BRIDGE

London Bridge is falling down,
Falling down, falling down,
London Bridge is falling down,
My fair lady.

Build it up with wood and clay,
Wood and clay, wood and clay,
Build it up with wood and clay,
My fair lady.

LUCY LOCKET

Lucy Locket
Lost her pocket,
Kitty Fisher found it.
Nothing in it,
Nothing in it,
But the binding round it.

GEORGIE PORGIE

Georgie Porgie,
  pudding and pie,
Kissed the girls
  and made them cry.
When the boys
  came out to play,
Georgie Porgie ran away.

ONE, TWO, THREE

One, two, three,
Four and five,
I caught a hare alive,
Six, seven, eight,
Nine and ten,
I let him go again.

LITTLE JUMPING JOAN

Here am I,
Little jumping Joan.
When nobody's with me,
I'm always alone.

I SENT A LETTER TO MY LOVE

I sent a letter to my love
And on the way I dropped it,
A little puppy picked it up
And put it in his pocket.

WHERE HAS MY
LITTLE DOG GONE

Oh, where, oh, where
Has my little dog gone?
Oh, where, oh, where can he be?
With his ears cut short
And his tail cut long,
Oh, where, oh, where can he be?

LILIES ARE WHITE

Lilies are white,
Rosemary's green,
When you are king,
I will be queen.
Roses are red,
Lavender's blue,
If you will have me,
I will have you.

CURLY LOCKS!

Curly Locks! Curly Locks!
Will you be mine?
You shall not wash dishes
Nor feed the swine,
But sit on a cushion
And sew a fine seam,
And feed upon strawberries,
Sugar and cream.

TOMMY SNOOKS AND BESSY BROOKS

As Tommy Snooks
  and Bessy Brooks
Were walking out on Sunday,
Said Tommy Snooks
  to Bessy Brooks,
"Tomorrow will be Monday."

BOBBY SHAFTOE

Bobby Shaftoe's gone to sea,
Silver buckles on his knee,
He'll come back and marry me,
Pretty Bobby Shaftoe.
Bobby Shaftoe's fat and fair,
Combing down his auburn hair,
He's my love for evermore,
Pretty Bobby Shaftoe.

WEE WILLIE WINKIE

Wee Willie Winkie runs through the town
Upstairs and downstairs in his nightgown,
Rapping at the window,
Crying through the lock,
"Are the children in their beds,
For now it's eight o'clock?"

PEASE-PORRIDGE HOT

Pease-porridge hot,
Pease-porridge cold,
Pease-porridge in the pot,
Nine days old.
Some like it hot,
Some like it cold,
Some like it in the pot,
Nine days old.

JACK, BE NIMBLE

Jack, be nimble,
Jack, be quick,
Jack, jump over
The candlestick.

HICKORY, DICKORY, DOCK

Hickory, dickory, dock,
The mouse ran up the clock!
The clock struck one
And down he ran,
Hickory, dickory, dock.

DEEDLE, DEEDLE, DUMPLING

Deedle, deedle, dumpling,
My son John
Went to bed
With his stockings on —
One shoe off
And one shoe on —
Deedle, deedle, dumpling,
My son John.

RIDE A FAST HORSE

Ride a fast horse
   to Banbury Cross
To see a fine lady upon a
   white horse,

Rings on her fingers and bells
   on her toes,
She shall have music wherever
   she goes.

HARK, HARK,
THE DOGS DO BARK

Hark, hark, the dogs do bark!
The beggars are coming to town.
Some in rags and some in tags,
And one in a velvet gown.

YANKEE DOODLE

Yankee Doodle went to town
Riding on a pony,
Stuck a feather in his hat
And called it Macaroni.

LITTLE MISS LILY

Little Miss Lily, you're
  dreadfully silly
To wear such a very long skirt.
If you take my advice,
You would hold it up nice,
And not let it trail in the dirt.

DAFFY-DOWN-DILLY

Daffy-Down-Dilly
Has come up to town
In a yellow petticoat
And a green gown.

THE MUFFIN MAN

"Oh, do you know the muffin man,
The muffin man, the muffin man,
Oh, do you know the muffin man
Who lives in Drury Lane?"
"Oh yes, I know the muffin man,
The muffin man, the muffin man,
Oh yes, I know the muffin man
Who lives in Drury Lane."

HOT-CROSS BUNS

Hot-cross buns!
Hot-cross buns!
One a penny, two a penny,
Hot-cross buns!
If you have no daughters,
Give them to your sons.
One a penny, two a penny,
Hot-cross buns!

OLD CHAIRS TO MEND

If I'd as much money
As I could spend,
I never would cry,
"Old chairs to mend,
Old chairs to mend,
Old chairs to mend!"
I never would cry,
"Old chairs to mend!"

SMILING GIRLS,
ROSY BOYS

Smiling girls, rosy boys,
Come and buy my little toys,
Monkeys made of gingerbread,
And sugar horses painted red.

TOM, TOM,
THE PIPER'S SON

Tom, Tom, the piper's son,
Stole a pig and away did run!
The pig was eat
And Tom was beat
Till he ran crying
    down the street.

HIPPETY HOP
TO THE BARBER SHOP

Hippety hop
  to the barber shop
To get a stick of candy,
One for you
  and one for me,
And one for Sister Mandy.

COBBLER, COBBLER,
MEND MY SHOE

Cobbler, cobbler,
  mend my shoe,
And get it done
  by half past two.
If by half past two
It can't be done,
Get it done by half past one.

HANDY SPANDY

Handy spandy, Jack-a-dandy
Loved plum cake
   and sugar candy.
He bought some at
   a grocer's shop,
And out he came —
   hop, hop, hop.

PAT-A-CAKE

Pat-a-cake, pat-a-cake,
Baker's man.
Bake me a cake
As fast as you can.
Pat it and prick it,
And mark it with B,
And put it in the oven
For Baby and me.

LITTLE BETTY BLUE

Little Betty Blue
Lost her holiday shoe.
What will poor Betty do?
Why, give her another
To match the other
And then she may
    walk in two.

I'LL SING YOU A SONG

I'll sing you a song,
Though not very long,
Yet I think it's as pretty as any.
Put your hand in your purse,
You'll never be worse,
And give the poor singer
    a penny.

LET'S GO TO THE FAIR

Come on, let's go to the fair,
What shall we have when
    we get there?
A penny apple and a penny pear,
    Come on, let's go to the fair.

SIMPLE SIMON

Simple Simon met a pieman
Going to the Fair.
Said Simple Simon
    to the pieman,
"Let me taste your ware."
Said the pieman
    to Simple Simon,
"Show me first your penny."
Said Simple Simon
    to the pieman,
"Indeed, I haven't any."

WHAT CAN THE MATTER BE

Oh dear, what can the matter be?
Oh dear, what can the matter be?
Johnny's so long at the Fair.
He promised to buy me a bunch
    of blue ribbons,
He promised to buy me a bunch
    of blue ribbons,
To tie up my bonny brown hair.

JACK AND JILL

Jack and Jill went up the hill
To fetch a pail of water,
Jack fell down
And broke his crown,
And Jill came tumbling after.

THERE WAS AN OLD WOMAN LIVED UNDER A HILL

There was an old woman
Lived under a hill,
And if she's not gone
She lives there still.

BLOW, WIND, BLOW

Blow, wind, blow and go, mill, go
That the miller may grind his corn,
That the baker may take it,
And into bread make it,
And send us some
    hot in the morn.

THERE WAS A JOLLY MILLER

There was a jolly miller
Lived on the river Dee,
He worked and sang
From morn till night —
No one as gay as he.
And the song that he would sing
Forever used to be:
"I care for nobody,
No, not I,
And nobody cares for me."

LITTLE BOY BLUE

Little Boy Blue,
Come blow your horn,
The sheep's in the meadow,
The cow's in the corn.
But where is the little boy
Who looks after the sheep?
He's under the haystack
Fast asleep.
Will you wake him?
No, not I!
For if I do,
He's sure to cry.

BAA, BAA, BLACK SHEEP

"Baa, baa, black sheep,
Have you any wool?"
"Yes sir, yes sir,
Three bags full:
One for my master,
One for my dame,
And one for the little boy
Who lives down the lane."

LITTLE MAID, PRETTY MAID

"Little maid, pretty maid,
Where goest thou?"
"Down in the meadow
To milk my cow."
"Shall I go with thee?"
"No, not now!
When I send for thee,
Then come thou."

MARY HAD A LITTLE LAMB

Mary had a little lamb,
Its fleece was white as snow,
And everywhere that Mary went
The lamb was sure to go.
It followed her to school one day,
Which was against the rule.
It made the children laugh and play
To see a lamb at school.

LITTLE BO PEEP

Little Bo Peep has lost her sheep
And can't tell where to find them.
Leave them alone,
And they'll come home,
Wagging their tails behind them.

HICKETY PICKETY

Hickety pickety, my fat hen,
She lays eggs for gentlemen,
Sometimes nine
   and sometimes ten,
Hickety pickety, my fat hen.

CACKLE, CACKLE, MADAM GOOSE

"Cackle, cackle, Madam Goose!
Have you any feathers loose?"
"Yes, I have, little fellow,
Half enough to fill a pillow."

DICKERY, DICKERY, DARE

Dickery, dickery, dare,
The pig flew up in the air.
The man in brown
Soon brought him down,
Dickery, dickery, dare.

LITTLE MISS MUFFET

Little Miss Muffet
Sat on a tuffet,
Eating her curds and whey.
Along came a spider
Who sat down beside her,
And frightened
 Miss Muffet away.

LADYBUG, LADYBUG

Ladybug, ladybug,
Fly away home,
Your house is on fire,
Your children will roam.

BOW WOW, SAYS THE DOG

"Bow wow," says the dog,
"Meow," says the cat,
"Grunt, grunt," goes the hog,
"And squeak," says the rat.
"Who, who," says the owl,
"Caw, caw," says the crow,
"Quack, quack," goes the duck,
And "Moo," says the cow.

WOULDN'T IT BE FUNNY

Wouldn't it be funny —
Wouldn't it now —
If the dog said, "Moo,"
And the cow said, "Bow wow?"
If the cat sang and whistled,
And the bird said, "Meow?"
Wouldn't it be funny —
Wouldn't it now?

I LIKE LITTLE PUSSY

I like little Pussy,
Her coat is so warm,
And if I don't hurt her
She'll do me no harm.
So I'll not pull her tail,
Nor drive her away,
But Pussy and I
Very gently will play.

DING, DONG, BELL

Ding, dong, bell,
Pussy's in the well!
Who put her in?
Little Johnny Green.
Who pulled her out?
Little Tommy Stout.
What a naughty boy was that
To try to drown poor Pussy Cat,
Who never once did any harm,
And caught the mice
    in Father's barn.

DIDDLEDY, DIDDLEDY, DUMPTY

Diddledy, diddledy, dumpty,
The cat ran up the plum tree.
Half a crown
To fetch her down,
Diddledy, diddledy, dumpty.

PUSSY CAT, PUSSY CAT

"Pussy Cat, Pussy Cat,
Where have you been?"
"I've been to London
To visit the Queen."
"Pussy Cat, Pussy Cat,
What did you there?"
"I frightened a little mouse
Under her chair."

45

ONCE I SAW A LITTLE BIRD

Once I saw a little bird
Come hop, hop, hop!
And I cried, "Little bird,
Please stop, stop, stop!"
I was going to the window
To say, "How do you do?"
But he shook his little tail,
And away he flew.

TWO LITTLE BLACKBIRDS

Two little blackbirds
Sitting on a hill —
One named Jack,
The other named Jill.
Fly away, Jack,
Fly away, Jill.
Come back, Jack,
Come back, Jill.

I HAD TWO BIRDIES

I had two birdies bright and gay,
They flew from me the other day.
What was the reason they did go?
I cannot tell for I do not know.

THE NORTH WIND WILL BLOW

The north wind will blow
And we shall have snow,
And what will poor Robin
   do then?
Poor thing!
He'll sit in the barn
And keep himself warm,
And hide his head under
   his wing.
Poor thing!

47

I'M GLAD THE SKY IS PAINTED BLUE

I'm glad the sky is painted blue,
And earth is painted green,
With such a lot of nice fresh air
All sandwiched inbetween.

MARY, MARY, QUITE CONTRARY

Mary, Mary, quite contrary,
How does your garden grow?
With silver bells,
And cockleshells,
And pretty maids all in a row.

RABBIT, RABBIT, CARROT-EATER

Rabbit, Rabbit, carrot-eater,
Says he, "There is nothing
      sweeter
Than a carrot every day —
Munch and crunch
      and run away."

PETER PIPER

Peter Piper picked
A peck of pickled peppers,
A peck of pickled peppers
Peter Piper picked.
If Peter Piper picked
A peck of pickled peppers,
Where's the peck of pickled
      peppers
Peter Piper picked?

LITTLE JACK PUMPKIN FACE

Little Jack Pumpkin Face
Lived on a vine,
Little Jack Pumpkin Face
Thought it was fine.

First he was small and green,
Then big and yellow,
Little Jack Pumpkin Face
Is a fine fellow.

PETER, PETER, PUMPKIN-EATER

Peter, Peter, pumpkin-eater,
Had a wife and couldn't keep her.
He put her in a pumpkin shell
And there he kept her very well.

UP IN GREEN ORCHARD

Up in Green Orchard
There is a green tree,
The finest of pippins
You ever did see!
The apples are ripe
And ready to fall,
And Reuben and Robin
Shall gather them all.

IF I WERE AN APPLE

If I were an apple
And grew on a tree,
I think I'd drop down
On a nice boy like me.
I wouldn't stay there
Giving nobody joy,
I'd fall down at once
And say, "Eat me, my boy!"

TOM, HE WAS A PIPER'S SON

Tom, he was a piper's son,
He learned to play when he was young,
But the only tune that he could play
Was "Over the hills and far away.
Over the hills and a great way off,
And the wind will blow my topknot off."

A DILLER, A DOLLAR

A diller, a dollar,
A ten o'clock scholar,
What makes you come so soon?
You used to come at ten o'clock,
And now you come at noon.

SING A SONG OF SIXPENCE

Sing a song of sixpence,
A pocket full of rye,
Four and twenty blackbirds
Baked in a pie.

When the pie was opened,
The birds began to sing.
Wasn't that a dainty dish
To set before the king?

The king was in the counting house
Counting out his money.
The queen was in the parlor
Eating bread and honey.

The maid was in the garden
Hanging up the clothes.
Along came a blackbird,
And pecked off her nose.

HUMPTY DUMPTY

Humpty Dumpty sat on a wall,
Humpty Dumpty had a great fall.
All the king's horses
And all the king's men
Couldn't put Humpty together again.

THE QUEEN OF HEARTS

The Queen of Hearts,
She made some tarts
All on a summer's day.
The Knave of Hearts,
He stole the tarts
And took them clean
   away.

The King of Hearts
Called for the tarts
And beat the Knave
   full sore.
The Knave of Hearts
Brought back the tarts
And vowed he'd steal
   no more.

OLD KING COLE

Old King Cole
   was a merry old soul,
And a merry old soul was he,
He called for his pipe,
And he called for his bowl,
And he called
   for his fiddlers three.

Every fiddler,
   he had a fiddle,
And a very fine fiddle had he,
Oh, there's none so rare
As can compare
With King Cole
   and his fiddlers three.

HEY DIDDLE DIDDLE

Hey! diddle, diddle!
The cat and the fiddle,
The cow jumped over the moon.
The little dog laughed
To see such sport,
And the dish ran away with the spoon.

LITTLE JACK HORNER

Little Jack Horner
Sat in a corner,
Eating his Christmas pie.
He put in his thumb
And pulled out a plum,
And said,
   "What a good boy am I!"

OLD MOTHER HUBBARD

Old Mother Hubbard
Went to the cupboard
To get her poor dog a bone,
But when she got there
The cupboard was bare
And so the poor dog had none.

JACK SPRAT
Jack Sprat could eat no fat,
His wife could eat no lean,
And so, between the two of them,
They licked the platter clean.

THERE WAS A CROOKED MAN

There was a crooked man
Who walked a crooked mile,
He found a crooked sixpence
Against a crooked stile.
He bought a crooked cat,
Which caught a crooked mouse,
And they all lived together
In a little crooked house.

THERE WAS AN OLD WOMAN
WHO LIVED IN A SHOE

There was an old woman
Who lived in a shoe,
She had so many children
She didn't know what to do.
She gave them some broth
Without any bread,
And spanked them all soundly
And sent them to bed.

THERE WAS AN OLD WOMAN WHO LIVED BY THE SEA

There was an old woman
Who lived by the sea,
And she was as merry
As merry could be!
She did nothing but carol
From morning till night,
And sometimes she caroled
By candlelight.
She caroled in time
And she caroled in tune,
But none cared to hear
But the man in the moon.

TWINKLE, TWINKLE, LITTLE STAR

Twinkle, twinkle, little star;
How I wonder what you are!
Up above the world so high,
Like a diamond in the sky.

RUB-A-DUB-DUB

Rub-a-dub-dub,
Three men in a tub,
And who do you think they be?
The butcher, the baker,
The candlestick maker,
They've all gone off on a spree.

STAR LIGHT, STAR BRIGHT

Star light, star bright,
First star I see tonight,
I wish I may, I wish I might,
Have the wish I wish tonight.

IF ALL THE WORLD

If all the world were apple pie
And all the sea were ink,
And all the trees were bread and cheese,
What would we have to drink?
It's enough to make an old man
Scratch his head and think!

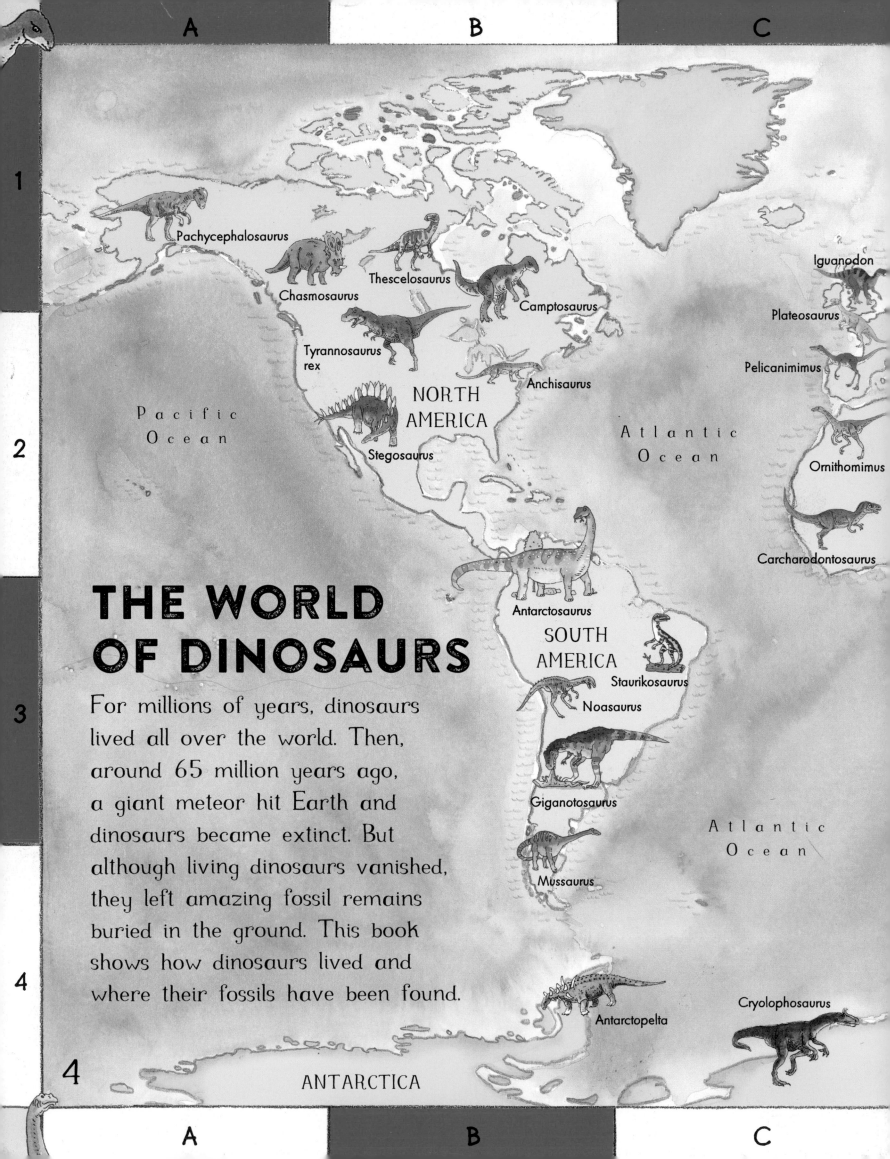

THE WORLD OF DINOSAURS

For millions of years, dinosaurs lived all over the world. Then, around 65 million years ago, a giant meteor hit Earth and dinosaurs became extinct. But although living dinosaurs vanished, they left amazing fossil remains buried in the ground. This book shows how dinosaurs lived and where their fossils have been found.

NORTH AMERICA

SOUTH AMERICA

ANTARCTICA

Pacific Ocean

Atlantic Ocean

Atlantic Ocean

Pachycephalosaurus

Chasmosaurus

Thescelosaurus

Camptosaurus

Tyrannosaurus rex

Anchisaurus

Stegosaurus

Iguanodon

Plateosaurus

Pelicanimimus

Ornithomimus

Carcharodontosaurus

Antarctosaurus

Staurikosaurus

Noasaurus

Giganotosaurus

Mussaurus

Antarctopelta

Cryolophosaurus

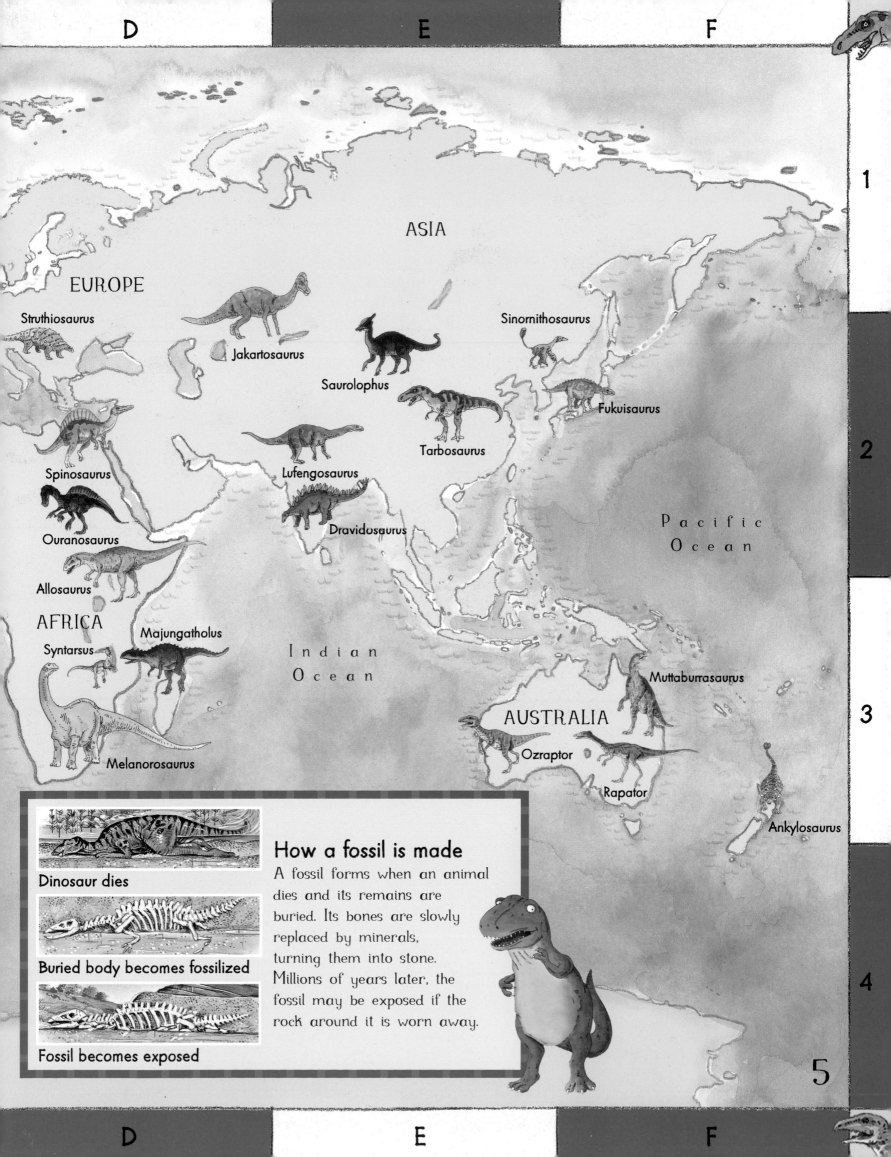

ASIA

EUROPE

Struthiosaurus

Jakartosaurus

Saurolophus

Sinornithosaurus

Fukuisaurus

Spinosaurus

Lufengosaurus

Tarbosaurus

Ouranosaurus

Dravidosaurus

2

Pacific
Ocean

Allosaurus

AFRICA

Majungatholus

Syntarsus

Indian
Ocean

Muttaburrasaurus

AUSTRALIA

Ozraptor

Rapator

Melanorosaurus

Ankylosaurus

How a fossil is made

A fossil forms when an animal
dies and its remains are
buried. Its bones are slowly
replaced by minerals,
turning them into stone.
Millions of years later, the
fossil may be exposed if the
rock around it is worn away.

Dinosaur dies

Buried body becomes fossilized

Fossil becomes exposed

THE AGE OF DINOSAURS

Dinosaurs lived on Earth for more than 160 million years. Scientists split this time into three periods: Triassic, Jurassic and Cretaceous. During each period, many different dinosaurs evolved and died out. Earth's surface also changed as the continents slowly drifted apart into the seven continents that exist today.

Earth in the Cretaceous period

Compsognathus

Triassic

This period started 251 million years ago. At the beginning of the Triassic, most of the world's land was joined in a huge supercontinent called Pangaea.

6

Dinosaur hunters

The first dinosaur fossils were dug up in Europe in the 1800s. Since then, dinosaur hunters have found fossils on every continent, including Antarctica. The giant fossilized bones being uncovered here in Niger, Africa, are those of a large plant eater.

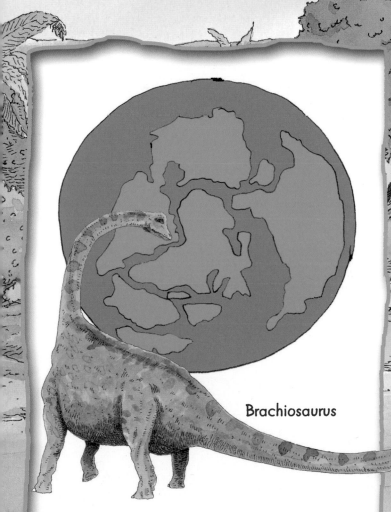

Brachiosaurus

Tyrannosaurus rex

Jurassic

This period started around 200 million years ago. In Jurassic times, Pangaea began to break apart. The continents drifted away from one another, taking the animals with them.

Cretaceous

This period began 145 million years ago. It ended 65 million years ago when a huge meteor struck Earth, wiping out the dinosaurs.

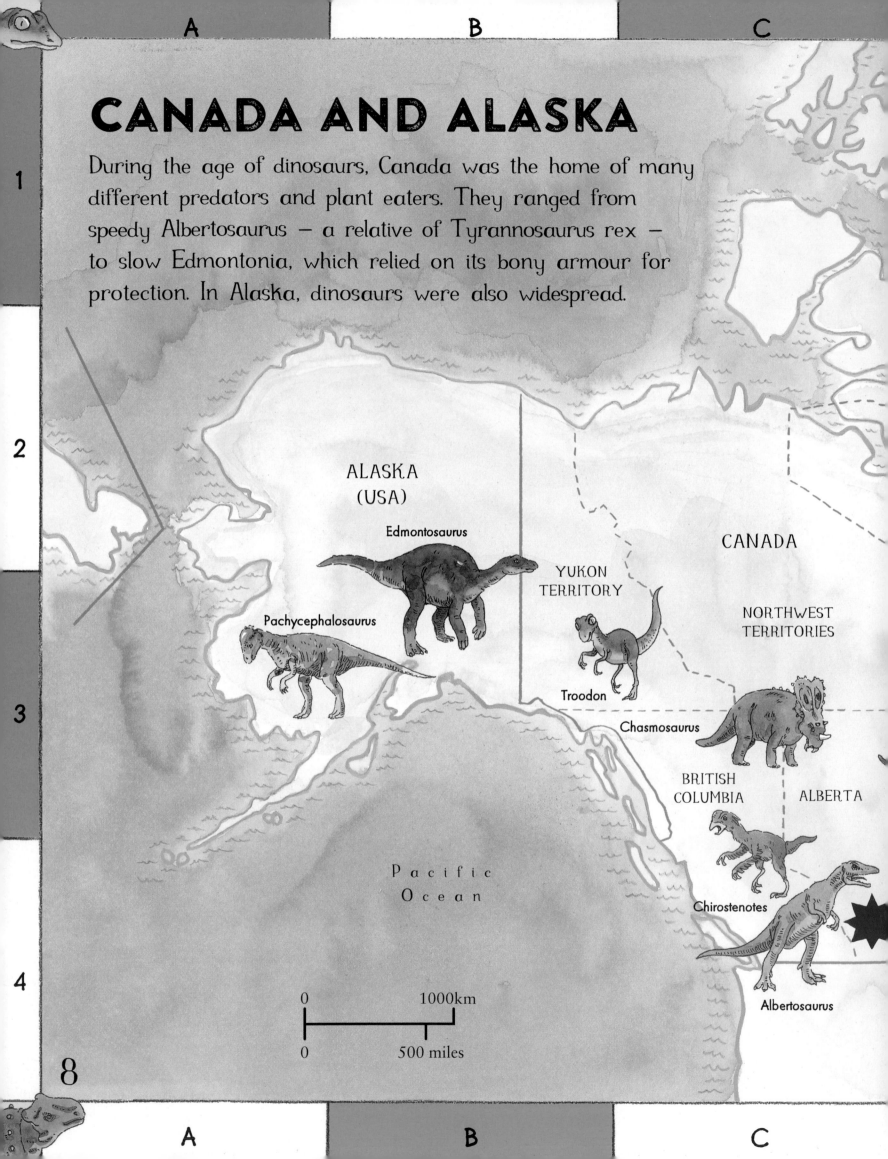

CANADA AND ALASKA

During the age of dinosaurs, Canada was the home of many different predators and plant eaters. They ranged from speedy Albertosaurus – a relative of Tyrannosaurus rex – to slow Edmontonia, which relied on its bony armour for protection. In Alaska, dinosaurs were also widespread.

ALASKA
(USA)

Edmontosaurus

Pachycephalosaurus

YUKON
TERRITORY

Troodon

CANADA

NORTHWEST
TERRITORIES

Chasmosaurus

BRITISH
COLUMBIA

ALBERTA

Chirostenotes

Pacific
Ocean

Albertosaurus

0   1000km

0   500 miles

8

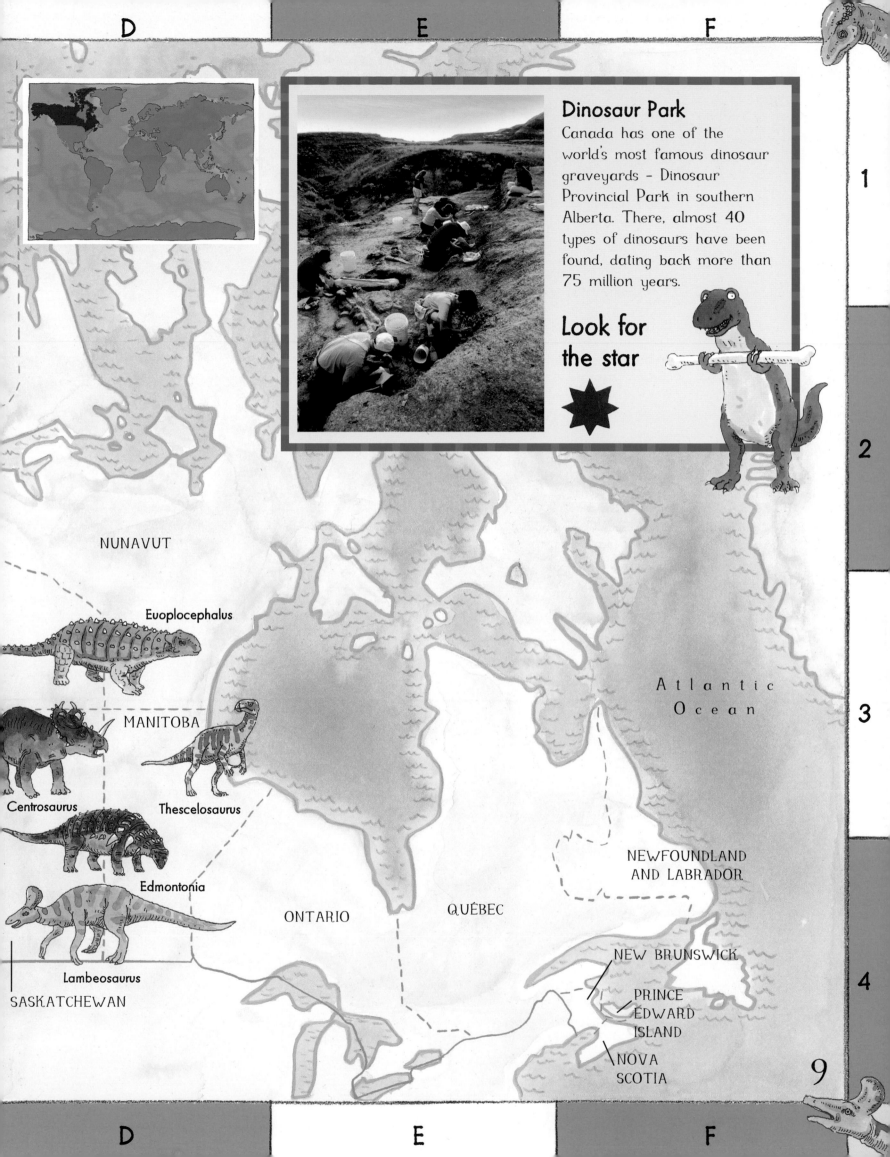

Dinosaur Park

Canada has one of the world's most famous dinosaur graveyards – Dinosaur Provincial Park in southern Alberta. There, almost 40 types of dinosaurs have been found, dating back more than 75 million years.

Look for the star

NUNAVUT

Euoplocephalus

MANITOBA

Centrosaurus

Thescelosaurus

Edmontonia

Lambeosaurus

SASKATCHEWAN

ONTARIO

QUÉBEC

Atlantic Ocean

NEWFOUNDLAND AND LABRADOR

NEW BRUNSWICK

PRINCE EDWARD ISLAND

NOVA SCOTIA

1

2

3

4

PACK ATTACK

In the age of dinosaurs, Canada was a much warmer place than it is today. It was covered by lush plants — making it a perfect feeding ground for Lambeosaurus, a duck-billed dinosaur with a large hollow crest on its head. Lambeosaurus had many enemies, including Dromaeosaurus, which hunted and attacked in groups.

Toothless wonder

Chirostenotes had a bony crest on its head and beak-shaped jaws without any teeth. It hunted smaller animals, pecking at them just like today's birds.

Lambeosaurus

Dromaeosaurus

10

Just for show

Chasmosaurus had a giant frill behind its head. Instead of being solid, the frill had a bony framework covered with skin. It might have been used to frighten off rivals or attract mates.

Night shift

Troodon had unusually large eyes, which may have helped it hunt at night. It probably chased small mammals that came out to feed when other dinosaurs were asleep.

THE UNITED STATES OF AMERICA

The USA's first complete dinosaur — a Hadrosaurus — was discovered in New Jersey in 1858. But most dinosaurs have been found further west. Dinosaur hunters have unearthed more than 120 types of dinosaurs, from giant plant eaters such as Diplodocus to Tyrannosaurus rex — probably the most famous dinosaur in the world.

Bone bed

The "dinosaur wall" at Dinosaur National Monument in Utah contains hundreds of dinosaur fossils on a ledge of sloping rock. This man is clearing rock, leaving the bones as they were found.

Look for the star

NORTH DAKOTA

Maiasaura

SOUTH DAKOTA

NEBRASKA

MINNESOTA

MICHIGAN

WISCONSIN

IOWA

Ceratosaurus

ILLINOIS

INDIANA

OHIO

PENNSYLVANIA

Coelophysis

MAINE

VERMONT

NEW HAMPSHIRE

NEW YORK

MASSACHUSETTS

RHODE ISLAND

Anchisaurus

CONNECTICUT

NEW JERSEY

Hadrosaurus

DELAWARE

KANSAS

MISSOURI

WEST VIRGINIA

MARYLAND

KENTUCKY

VIRGINIA

Apatosaurus

TENNESSEE

NORTH CAROLINA

OKLAHOMA   ARKANSAS

MISSISSIPPI

SOUTH CAROLINA

TEXAS

ALABAMA   GEORGIA

Stegoceras

LOUISIANA

Atlantic Ocean

FLORIDA

Gulf of Mexico

DINOSAUR NEST IN MONTANA

In the 1970s, dinosaur hunters made an incredible find in the mountains of Montana. As well as many fossilized dinosaur bones, they found nests, eggs and baby dinosaurs. The nests belonged to Maiasaura, or "good mother lizard". This plant-eating dinosaur laid up to 40 eggs in a mound-shaped nest and brought food to its young.

Maiasaura

Protoceratops
fossilized
eggs

Dinosaur eggs

Like reptiles today, most dinosaurs laid eggs. Compared to their size, dinosaur eggs were often quite small. Some were round, and others were long and narrow. These eggs were laid by Protoceratops, a dinosaur that lived in Mongolia (north-central Asia).

Growing up

When newly hatched, Maiasaura had a tiny skull and teeth that were smaller than a two-year-old child's. As it grew, its skull became bigger and longer, giving it a strong bite for crushing plants.

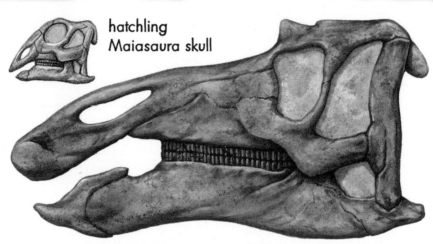

hatchling
Maiasaura skull

adult Maiasaura skull

15

NORTH AMERICAN DINOSAURS

Triceratops looked fierce, but it was actually a plant eater. It was up to four times as heavy as a rhinoceros, and its horns could be as much as a metre long. It used its horns to fight back against strong predators such as Tyrannosaurus rex.

Tyrannosaurus rex

Triceratops

King of the dinosaurs

Tyrannosaurus rex was one of the biggest two-legged predators, and it lived at the end of the age of dinosaurs. It ambushed smaller dinosaurs, but it also scavenged on the dead remains of other dinosaurs.

Tyrannosaurus rex

Scutellosaurus

Danger in numbers

Slim, lightweight and fast-moving, Deinonychus hunted in a pack. This dinosaur was able to catch and kill larger dinosaurs that moved too slowly to escape.

Tenontosaurus

Deinonychus

Deadly swing

Ankylosaurus had armoured skin and a tail club that weighed up to 45 kilograms (110 pounds). By swinging its club, it could smash open the skull of a large predator.

17

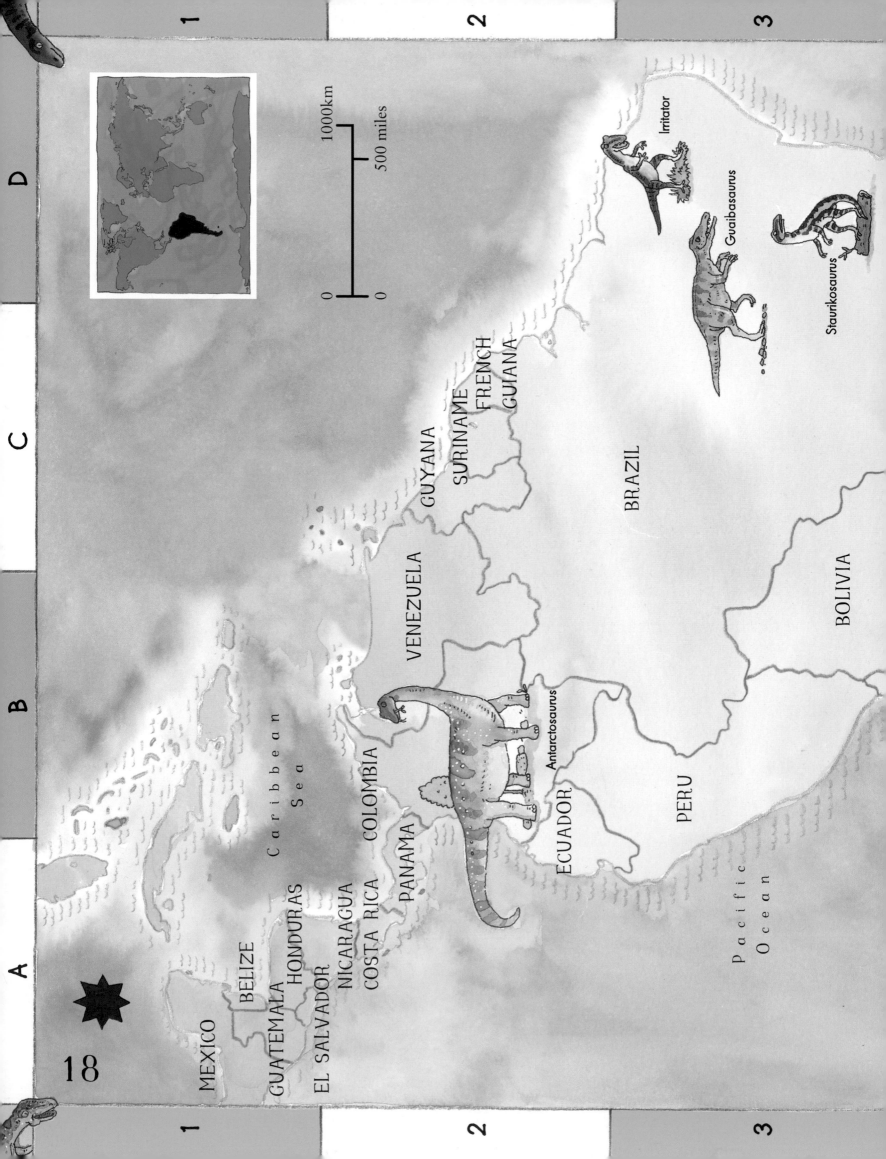

18

1   2   3

A   B   C   D

1000km
500 miles

0
0

MEXICO
BELIZE
GUATEMALA
HONDURAS
EL SALVADOR
NICARAGUA
COSTA RICA
PANAMA
COLOMBIA

Caribbean Sea

VENEZUELA
GUYANA
SURINAME
FRENCH GUIANA

ECUADOR

PERU

BRAZIL

BOLIVIA

Pacific Ocean

Antarctosaurus

Irritator

Guaibasaurus

Staurikosaurus

CENTRAL AND SOUTH AMERICA

Some of the world's earliest and biggest dinosaurs have been discovered in South America. These include Eoraptor, a chicken-size dinosaur that lived more than 225 million years ago, and Saltasaurus, a colossal plant eater that may have weighed almost 100 tons.

PARAGUAY

URUGUAY

ARGENTINA

CHILE

Saltasaurus

Herrerasaurus

Giganotosaurus

Noasaurus

Eoraptor

Argentinosaurus

Carnotaurus

Abelisaurus

Piatnitzkysaurus

Mussaurus

The crater is under the sea

Experts think that dinosaurs died out after a giant meteor crashed into Earth 65 million years ago. A huge crater has been found in the sea off the coast of Mexico, showing where the meteor might have struck.

Look for the star

19

DINOSAUR HUNTERS IN ARGENTINA

In Argentina's Valley of the Moon, scientists have found fossils of some of the earliest dinosaurs. One of them, Herrerasaurus, lived 228 million years ago. It was 6 metres (20 feet) long and hunted by running on its back legs.

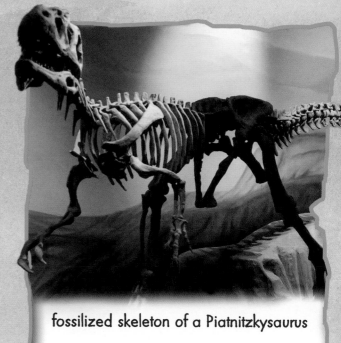

fossilized skeleton of a Piatnitzkysaurus

Out of reach
Like many hunting dinosaurs, Piatnitzkysaurus had huge back legs but tiny arms. It also had only three fingers on each of its hands.

Handy work

Eoraptor is another very early dinosaur that lived in the Valley of the Moon. Small and quick, it probably ate small animals as well as plants. It could hold the food it caught in its five-fingered hands.

Going to extremes

Giganotosaurus lived more than 100 million years after Herrerasaurus and Eoraptor. It was one of the biggest hunting dinosaurs, weighing as much as seven tons.

Herrerasaurus

Eoraptor

21

SOUTH AMERICAN DINOSAURS

Carnotaurus was one of the strangest dinosaurs from South America. Its skin was covered with knobby scales, and it had a small head, with a horn above each eye. It might have used the horns like bulls do when they fight rivals to win the right to mate with a female. The name Carnotaurus means "meat-eating bull".

fossilized skeleton of a baby Mussaurus

Tiny dino

The smallest complete dinosaur fossil is a baby Mussaurus from Argentina. It measures only 18 centimetres long. Mussaurus fed on plants. When fully grown, it probably grew to 5 metres (16 feet).

Carnotaurus

Tipping the scales

Saltasaurus was a plant eater that lived in Argentina. Its back was covered with hard bony plates, like those that protect today's crocodiles.

Slashing claw

Noasaurus might have had slashing claws on its hands. Measuring only $2\frac{1}{2}$ metres (8 feet) from head to tail, it would have been light enough to be able to leap on its prey.

23

EUROPE

In Europe, dinosaur fossils have been studied since the early 1800s, when naturalists figured out that they belonged to giant extinct reptiles. Since then, a huge variety of fossils have been found, including giant plant eaters such as Brachiosaurus and also Baryonyx – one of the few dinosaurs that ate mostly fish.

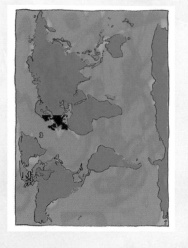

Early bird

Europe's fossils include many other prehistoric animals besides dinosaurs. The world's earliest known bird, called Archaeopteryx, was discovered in a limestone quarry in southern Germany. Around the size of a crow, it had teeth and a long, bony tail. However, it also had feathers and could fly.

Can you find Archaeopteryx?

fossilized skeleton of an Archaeopteryx

North Sea

NETHERLANDS

ENGLAND

WALES

UNITED KINGDOM

Megalosaurus

Eustreptospondylus

SCOTLAND

Saltosaurus

NORTHERN IRELAND

IRELAND

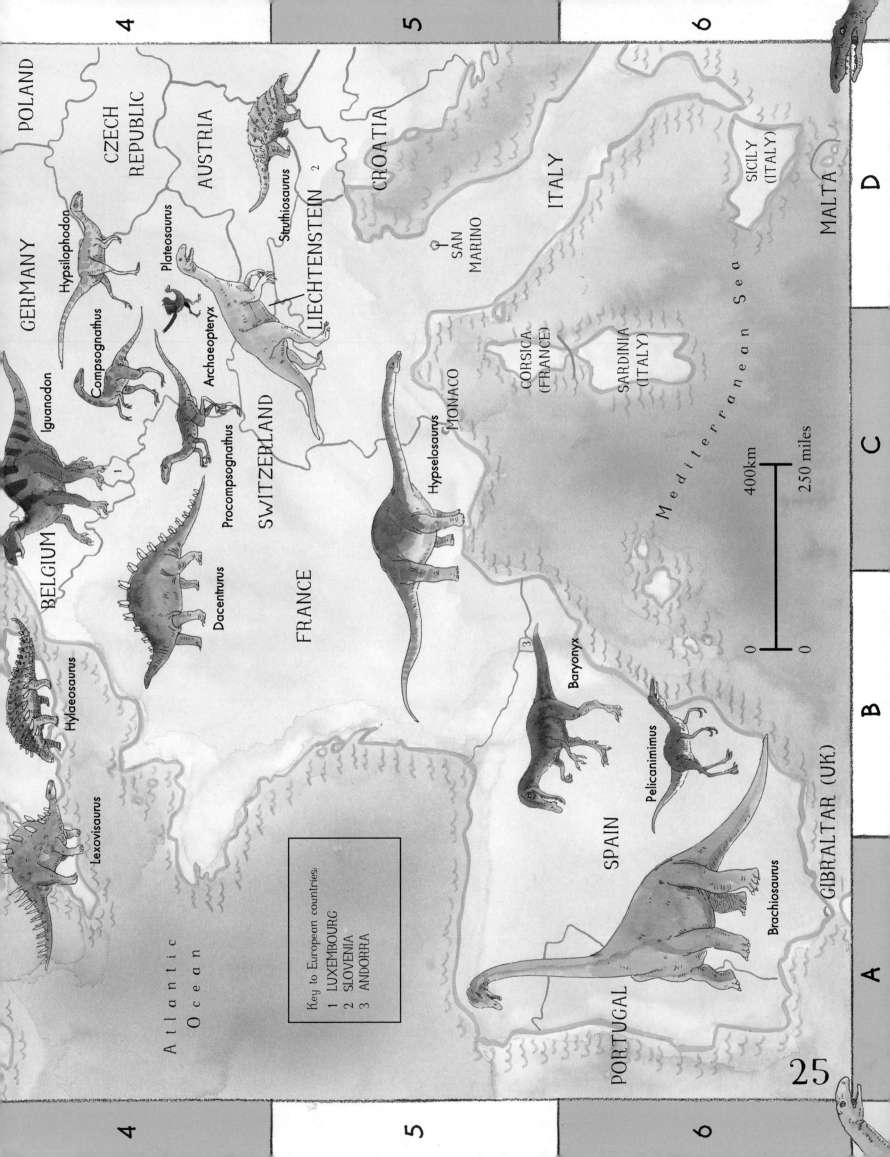

POLAND

GERMANY

CZECH
REPUBLIC

Hypsilophodon

AUSTRIA

Iguanodon

Compsognathus

Plateosaurus

Struthiosaurus

LIECHTENSTEIN ²

Archaeopteryx

CROATIA

Procompsognathus

SWITZERLAND

BELGIUM

ITALY

SAN
MARINO

Dacentrurus

Hylaeosaurus

FRANCE

MONACO

CORSICA
(FRANCE)

Hypselosaurus

Lexovisaurus

SARDINIA
(ITALY)

Mediterranean Sea

Atlantic
Ocean

400km

Key to European countries:
1 LUXEMBOURG
2 SLOVENIA
3 ANDORRA

250 miles

Baryonyx

0   0

SPAIN

Pelicanimimus

SICILY
(ITALY)

MALTA

Brachiosaurus

PORTUGAL

GIBRALTAR (UK)

4   5   6   C   B   A

4   5   6   D

DINOSAUR HERD IN BELGIUM

In 1878, a team of Belgian miners found 38 Iguanodon skeletons – the remains of a herd that lived more than 120 million years ago. The dinosaurs might have died when they tried to escape from predators, falling into a deep ravine.

fossilized Iguanodon skeletons

Iguanodon

Fossil herd

These skeletons of a Belgian Iguanodon herd are kept together in a museum. It is the largest display of a single type of dinosaur anywhere in the world.

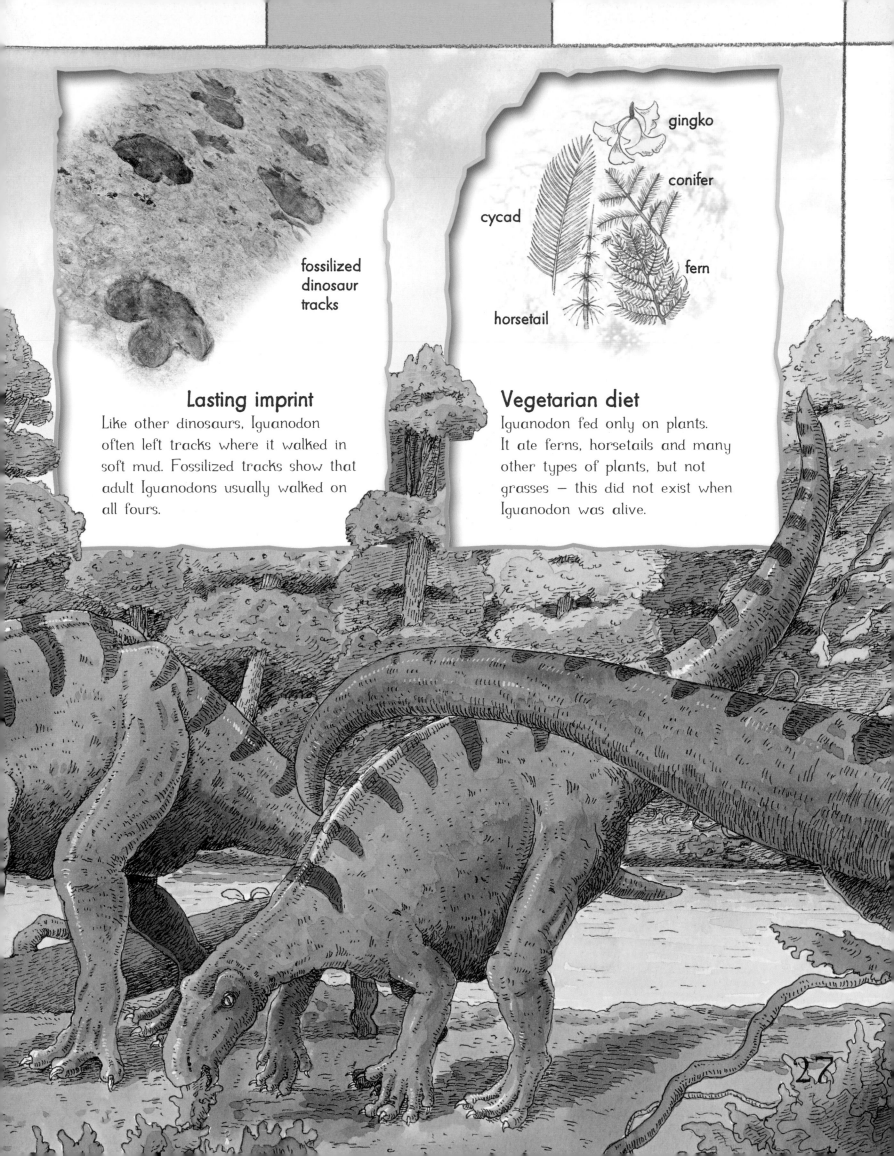

fossilized
dinosaur
tracks

gingko

conifer

cycad

fern

horsetail

Lasting imprint

Like other dinosaurs, Iguanodon
often left tracks where it walked in
soft mud. Fossilized tracks show that
adult Iguanodons usually walked on
all fours.

Vegetarian diet

Iguanodon fed only on plants.
It ate ferns, horsetails and many
other types of plants, but not
grasses — this did not exist when
Iguanodon was alive.

EUROPEAN DINOSAURS

Most dinosaurs fed on land, but Baryonyx was different. It had jaws like a crocodile's and long claws, especially on its thumbs. It probably waded into the shallows of rivers and lakes and caught fish as they swam past. One fossil of Baryonyx from southern England has fish bones and scales inside it.

Baryonyx

Feeding in the treetops

Brachiosaurus was up to 25 metres (82 feet) long, and its cranelike neck could reach almost twice as high as a giraffe's. It fed on leaves, tearing them off with its peg-shaped teeth. This sauropod lived in Europe, North America and Africa.

Little grinder

One of the smallest plant-eating dinosaurs, Hypsilophodon had a head the size of an adult human's hand. It fed on low-growing plants, grinding them up with its ridged teeth. It lived in herds and relied on its speed and sharp senses to escape danger, just like deer do today.

Chasing lizards

Compsognathus was a small, speedy dinosaur with a chicken-size body and a long neck and tail. It fed on lizards and other small animals, tearing them apart with its claws and teeth.

fossil of a
Hypsilophodon skull

29

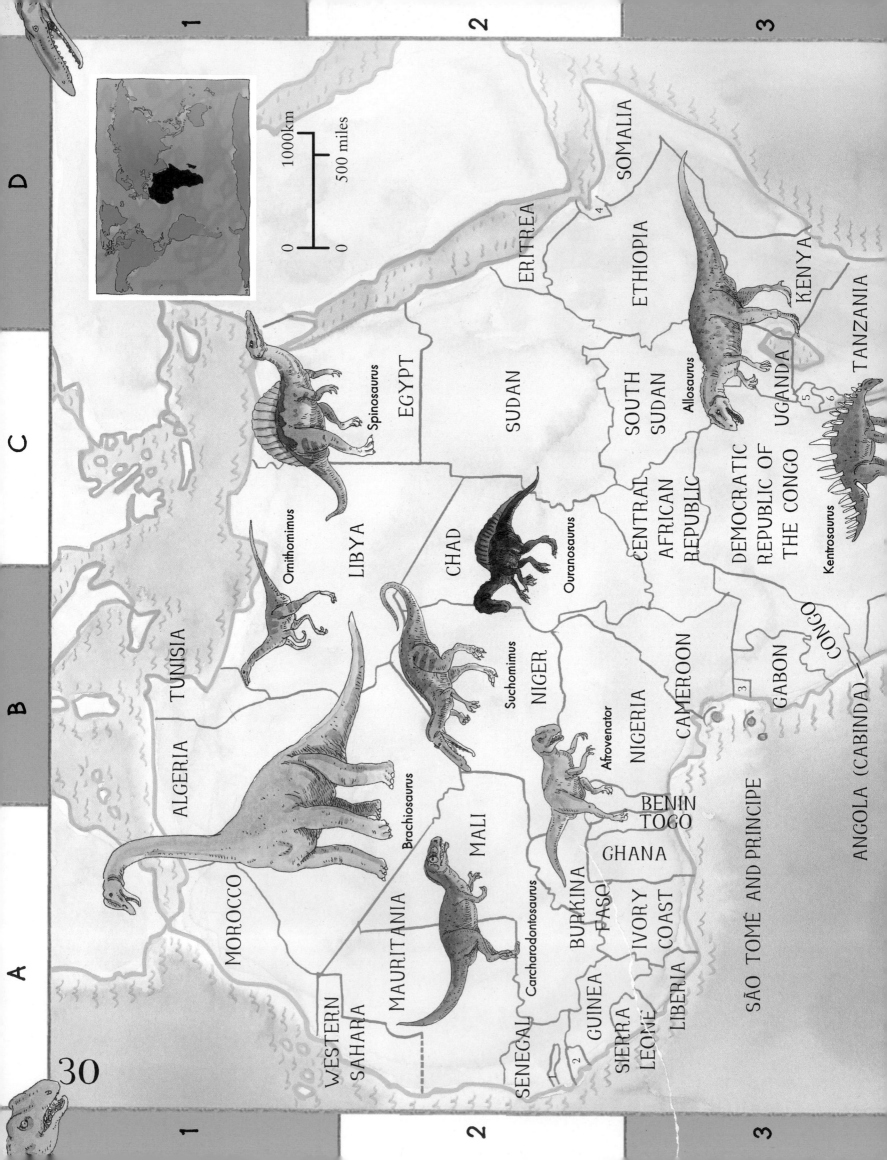

1

2

3

D

C

B

A

1000km

500 miles

0

0

MOROCCO

ALGERIA

TUNISIA

Ornithomimus

LIBYA

EGYPT

Spinosaurus

SUDAN

ERITREA

SOMALIA

ETHIOPIA

CHAD

Ouranosaurus

SOUTH
SUDAN

Allosaurus

KENYA

CENTRAL
AFRICAN
REPUBLIC

UGANDA

TANZANIA

DEMOCRATIC
REPUBLIC OF
THE CONGO

Kentrosaurus

WESTERN
SAHARA

MAURITANIA

Brachiosaurus

MALI

NIGER

Suchomimus

Afrovenator

CAMEROON

NIGERIA

GABON

CONGO

SENEGAL

Carcharodontosaurus

BURKINA
FASO

BENIN
TOGO

GHANA

IVORY
COAST

ANGOLA (CABINDA)

GUINEA

SIERRA
LEONE

LIBERIA

SÃO TOMÉ AND PRINCIPE

4

5

6

3

2

COMOROS

MADAGASCAR

MOZAMBIQUE

ZAMBIA

ANGOLA

NAMIBIA

SOUTH AFRICA

Ceratosaurus

Majungatholus

Vulcanodon

Syntarsus

Massospondylus

Melanorosaurus

Lesothosaurus

Heterodontosaurus

Euskelosaurus

7

8

9

10

11

Key to African countries:

1   THE GAMBIA
2   GUINEA-BISSAU
3   EQUATORIAL GUINEA
4   DJIBOUTI
5   RWANDA
6   BURUNDI
7   MALAWI
8   ZIMBABWE
9   BOTSWANA
10 ESWATINI
11 LESOTHO

AFRICA

Throughout Africa, dinosaur hunters have found fascinating fossils. They include some of the oldest dinosaurs, as well as the tallest and the most fearsome. Spinosaurus weighed almost twice as much as an African elephant, while Brachiosaurus towered over smaller plant-eating dinosaurs as it browsed the tops of trees.

Changing climate

In the Sahara Desert, dinosaur hunters unearth the fossilized remains of Afrovenator, a giant predator discovered in Niger in 1993. When the dinosaur was alive, the Sahara was damp and lush, with plenty of plant-eating prey.

Can you find Afrovenator?

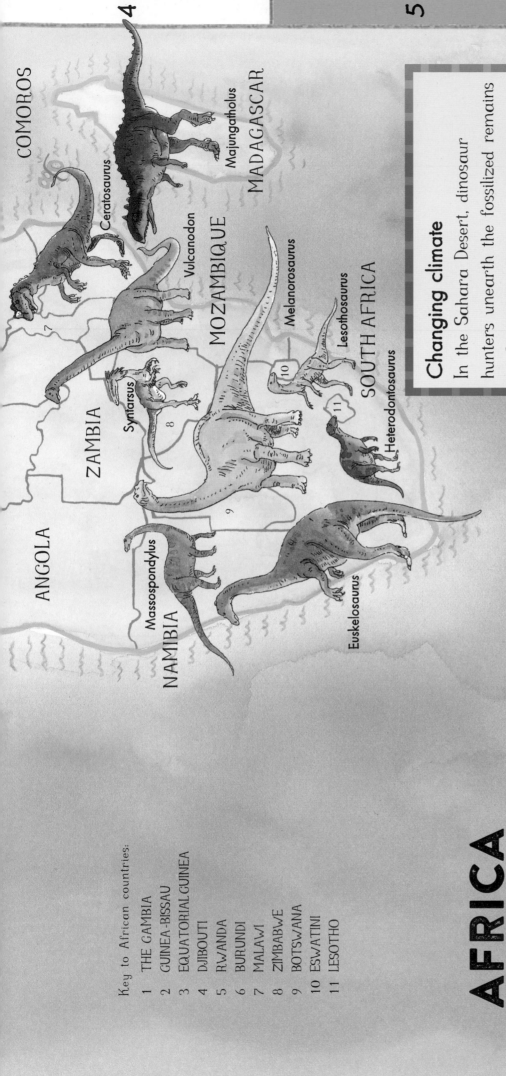

DUEL IN TANZANIA

In east Africa, a hungry Ceratosaurus tries to attack Kentrosaurus, a slow-moving plant eater. Kentrosaurus is smaller but is protected by bony plates and spikes that are up to 58 centimeters (23 inches) long. Each time the predator moves in, Kentrosaurus swivels around and lashes out with its tail.

Ceratosaurus

Kentrosaurus

Brachiosaurus

Big is best

Brachiosaurus relied on its size to stay out of danger. This enormous plant eater might have weighed up to 80 tons – much more than the biggest predators of its time. But when this giant got old and weak, it was easy prey to a Ceratosaurus.

Ceratosaurus

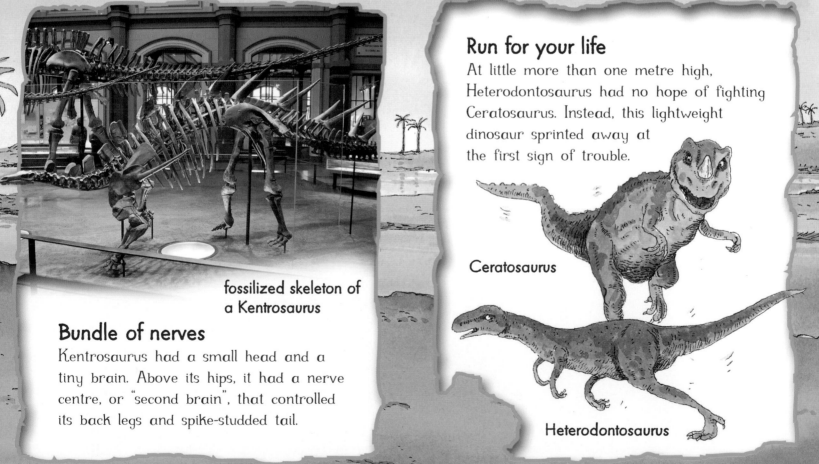

fossilized skeleton of a Kentrosaurus

Bundle of nerves

Kentrosaurus had a small head and a tiny brain. Above its hips, it had a nerve centre, or "second brain", that controlled its back legs and spike-studded tail.

Run for your life

At little more than one metre high, Heterodontosaurus had no hope of fighting Ceratosaurus. Instead, this lightweight dinosaur sprinted away at the first sign of trouble.

Ceratosaurus

Heterodontosaurus

33

AFRICAN DINOSAURS

Spinosaurus was one of the largest predatory dinosaurs, weighing as much as nine tons. In addition to having fearsome teeth and powerful jaws, it had a 2-metre- (6-foot-) high "sail". It might have used the sail like a solar panel, soaking up warmth at sunrise and sunset.

Spinosaurus

fossilized skull of a Carcharadontosaurus

Quick exit

Massopondylus lived around 190 million years ago, toward the beginning of the age of dinosaurs. It ate mostly plants and was lightweight. If danger threatened, it sped away on its back legs.

Giant bite

For pure biting power, few dinosaurs could match Carcharadontosaurus. Its skull was 1½ metres (5 feet) long. Its teeth had serrated edges — the biggest teeth were almost as long as a human skull.

Clever hunter

In 1993, researchers found the skeleton of an unknown dinosaur in the Sahara Desert. Although it was 125 million years old, the fossil was almost complete. Called Afrovenator — "African hunter" — it was around 9 metres (30 feet) long. It might have hunted fish in shallow water.

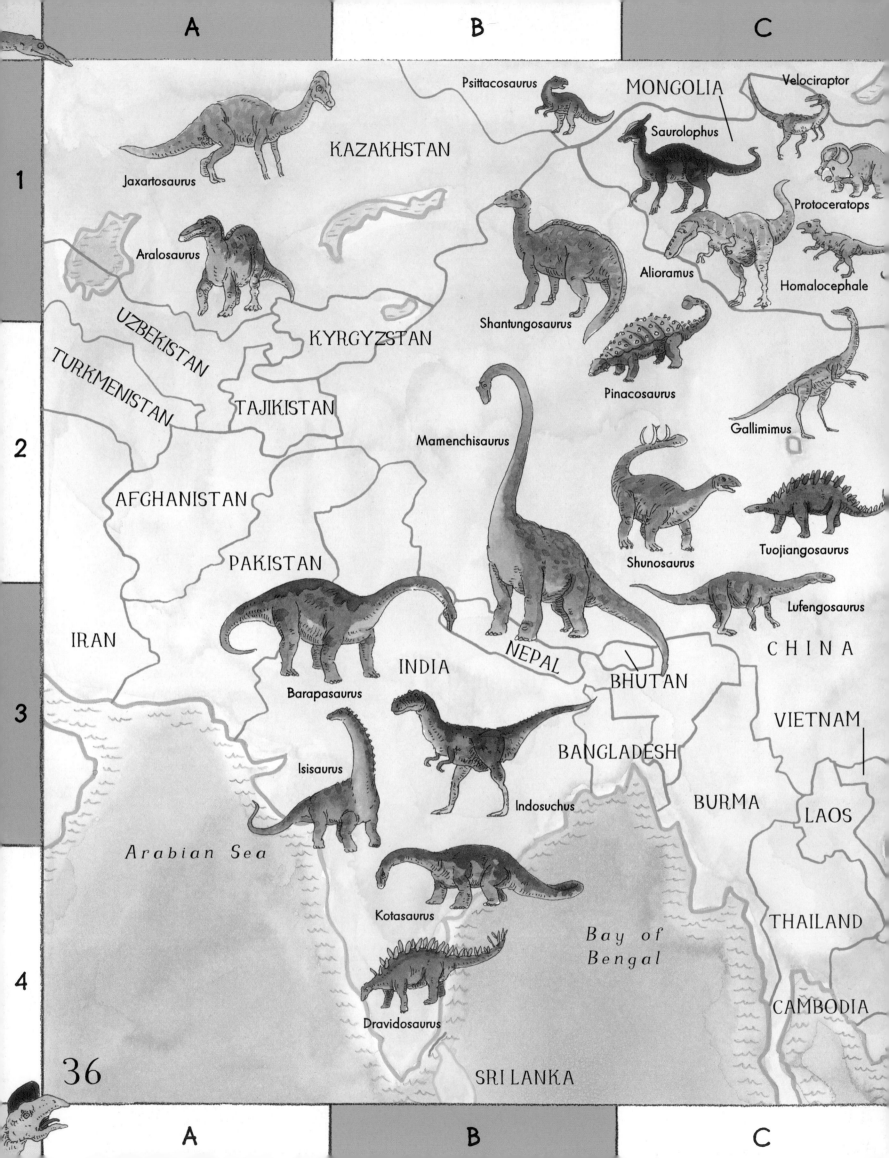

A B C

1

Psittacosaurus

MONGOLIA

Velociraptor

Saurolophus

KAZAKHSTAN

Jaxartosaurus

Protoceratops

Aralosaurus

Alioramus

Homalocephale

UZBEKISTAN

KYRGYZSTAN

Shantungosaurus

TURKMENISTAN

TAJIKISTAN

2

Mamenchisaurus

Pinacosaurus

Gallimimus

AFGHANISTAN

Shunosaurus

Tuojiangosaurus

PAKISTAN

CHINA

IRAN

Barapasaurus

Lufengosaurus

INDIA

NEPAL

BHUTAN

3

Isisaurus

BANGLADESH

VIETNAM

Indosuchus

BURMA

LAOS

Arabian Sea

Kotasaurus

Bay of Bengal

THAILAND

4

Dravidosaurus

CAMBODIA

36

SRI LANKA

A B C

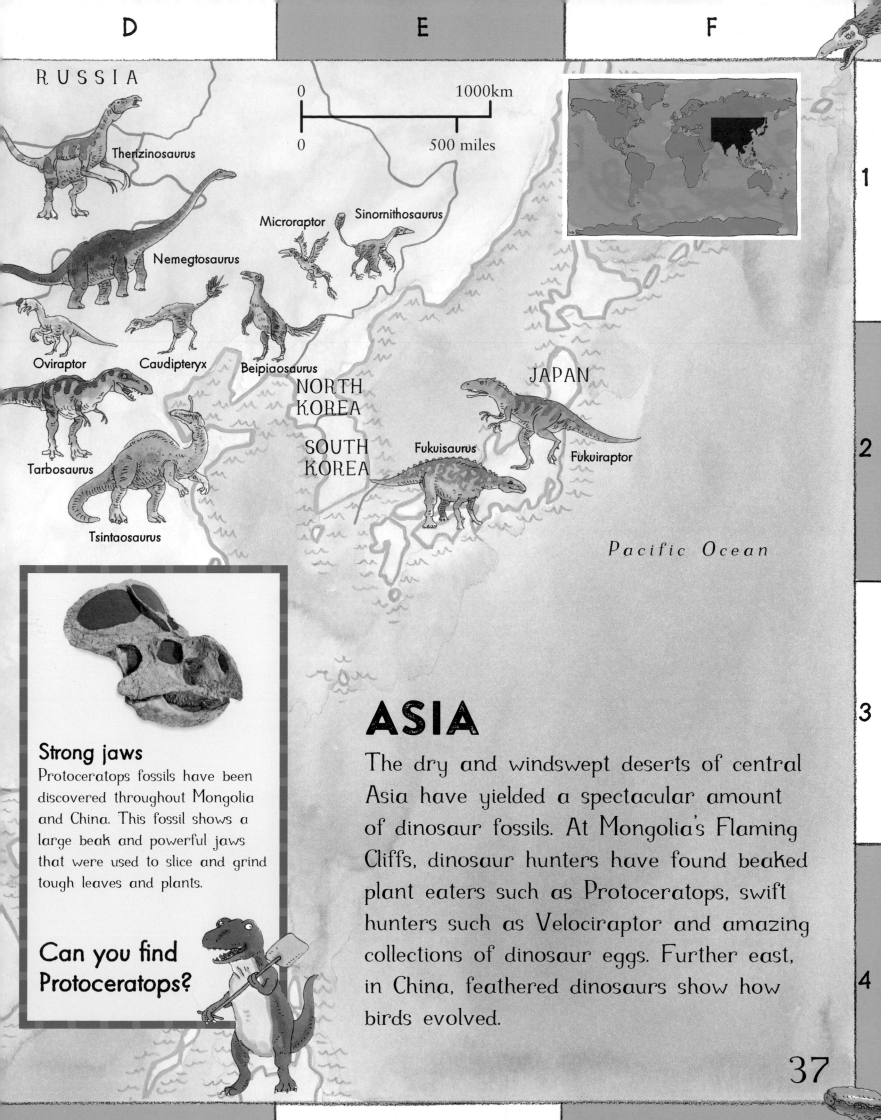

R U S S I A

Therizinosaurus

1000km

500 miles

Nemegtosaurus

Microraptor

Sinornithosaurus

Oviraptor

Caudipteryx

Beipiaosaurus

NORTH
KOREA

JAPAN

SOUTH
KOREA

Fukuisaurus

Fukuiraptor

Tarbosaurus

Tsintaosaurus

Pacific Ocean

1

2

3

4

Strong jaws

Protoceratops fossils have been discovered throughout Mongolia and China. This fossil shows a large beak and powerful jaws that were used to slice and grind tough leaves and plants.

Can you find Protoceratops?

ASIA

The dry and windswept deserts of central Asia have yielded a spectacular amount of dinosaur fossils. At Mongolia's Flaming Cliffs, dinosaur hunters have found beaked plant eaters such as Protoceratops, swift hunters such as Velociraptor and amazing collections of dinosaur eggs. Further east, in China, feathered dinosaurs show how birds evolved.

37

ASIAN DINOSAURS

Most of today's reptiles don't make any noise, but dinosaurs were very different. Saurolophus, from Asia and North America, made calls by inflating a pouch of skin that was above its snout. These calls would have filled the air when an entire Saurolophus herd spotted danger heading its way.

Large beak

Psittacosaurus, a plant eater, had a beak like a parrot's. It stood one metre high at the shoulder but was able to reach taller plants by standing on its back legs.

Tarbosaurus

Saurolophus

38

arms of a
Deinocheirus fossil

Scary claws

In the late 1960s, researcher in Mongolia found a huge pair of arm bones ending in 25-centimetre (10-inch) long claws. Very few other bones of their owner, Deinocheirus, have been found.

Nest raider

Gallimimus fed on the eggs and young of other dinosaurs, using its arms to dig and pick up food. Its long neck helped it spot food that was far away.

DINOSAUR FIGHT IN MONGOLIA

Velociraptor and Protoceratops were deadly enemies.
One fossil, found in the Gobi Desert, shows them locked
in combat. Velociraptor was attacking with its claws, while
Protoceratops hit back with its beak. They died suddenly,
probably because they were smothered by a sandstorm
or buried by a collapsing dune.

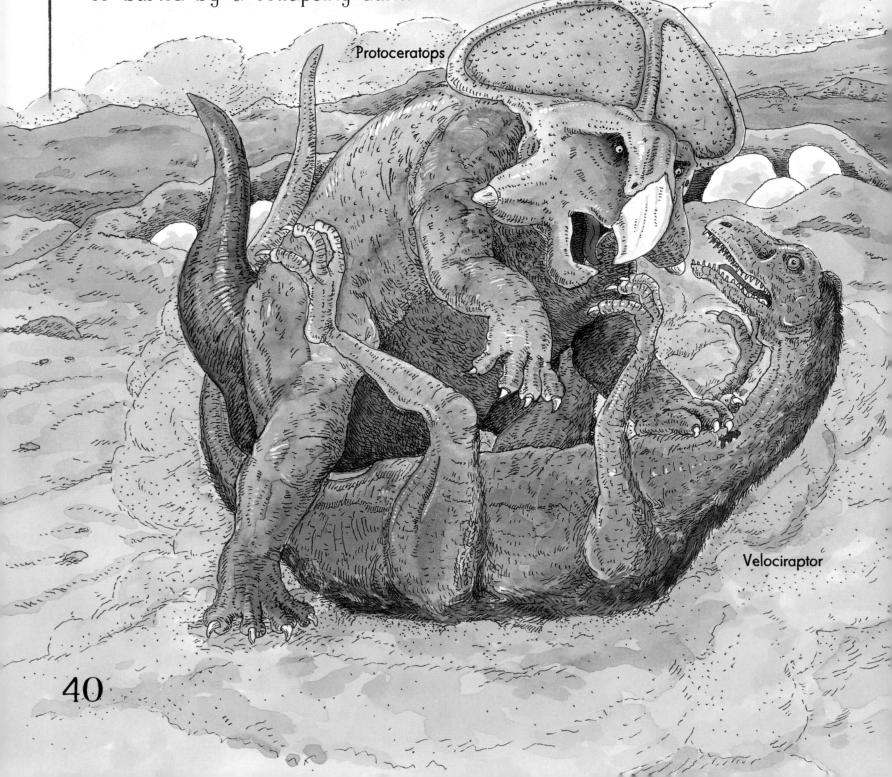

Protoceratops

Velociraptor

fossil of Oviraptor skeleton and eggs

Mother love

Some dinosaurs were very protective parents. This fossil is of an adult Oviraptor that died while sitting on its eggs. Inside each egg there are the tiny bones of the babies.

Low blows

The plant eater Pinacosaurus fought its enemies using a club on the end of its tail. By swinging the club close to the ground, it could smash a predator's legs, knocking it off its feet. Bony armour also helped keep it out of trouble.

Head-to-head collision

Homalocephale had an extra-thick layer of bone on the top of its skull. The males might have used this in head-butting contests, fighting to attract mates.

FEATHERED DINOSAURS OF CHINA

In Liaoning, in eastern China, researchers have found dinosaurs with fuzzy outlines of feathers instead of scaly skin. Some – including Caudipteryx – had feathers to stay warm. Others had bigger feathers and used them to fly. Scientists are certain that birds evolved from dinosaurs.

Caudipteryx

pointed scale

fluffy feather

feather with vanes

From scales to feathers

Feathers evolved gradually from hard, pointed scales. Fluffy feathers evolved first, helping keep dinosaurs warm. From these came much bigger feathers with branched vanes — the type that were inherited by the world's first true birds.

Ground attack

Protarchaeopteryx had long feathers on its arms, but it could not fly. It probably used its feathers like a scoop to catch insects and other small animals.

Winged flier

Microraptor was one of the smallest dinosaurs. It had feathers on its legs and arms, and it probably used all four limbs to fly. Instead of taking off from the ground, it might have jumped from trees.

AUSTRALIA AND NEW ZEALAND

Not many dinosaurs have been found in Australia. This is partly because most of Australia was covered by the ocean for most of the age of dinosaurs. Even so, Australia was the home of unusual dinosaurs, including the giant sauropod Austrosaurus and Minmi, an armoured dinosaur covered with bony plates.

Dinosaur trackway

AUSTRALIA

WESTERN AUSTRALIA

Dino tracks
Australia has some of the best preserved dinosaur trackways. One set, in Western Australia, contains giant footprints that are more than a metre wide.

Ozraptor

Can you find a trackway?

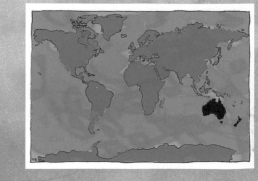

44

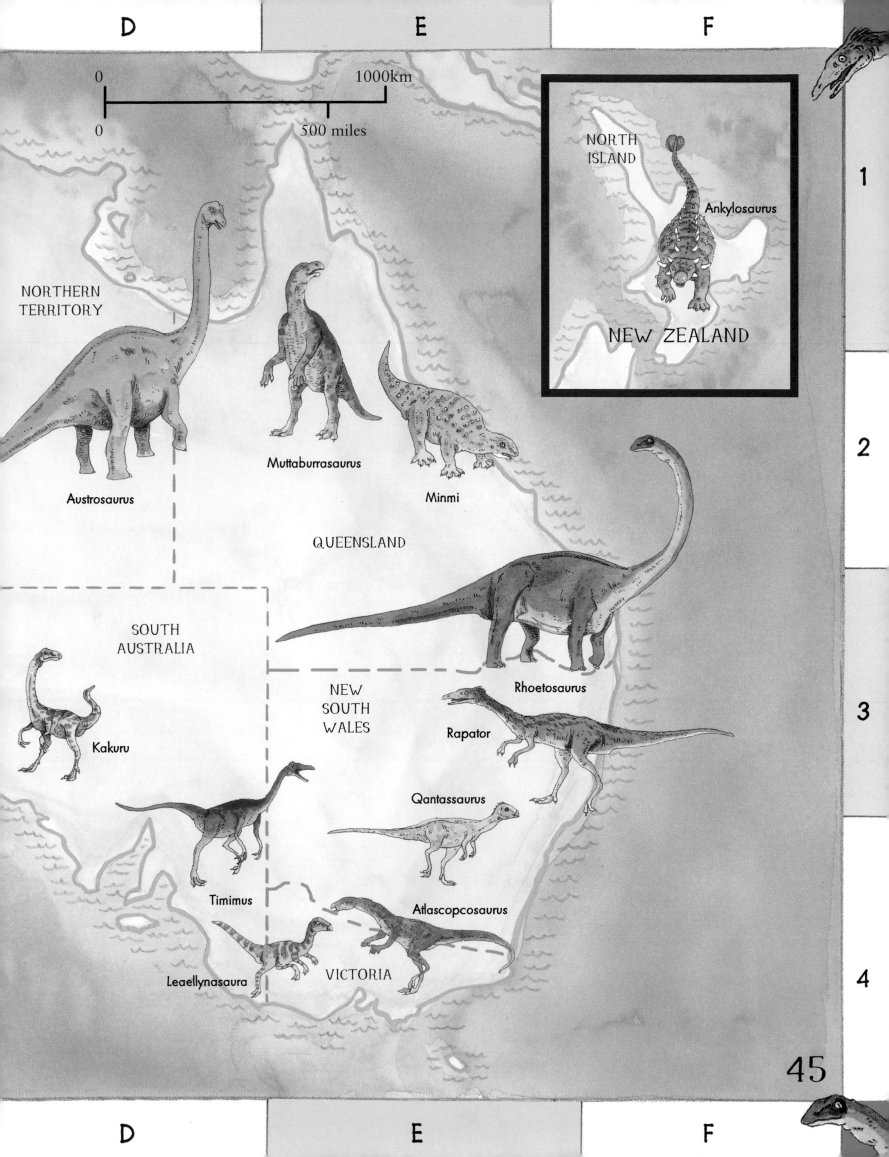

0
1000km

0
500 miles

NORTH
ISLAND

Ankylosaurus

NEW ZEALAND

NORTHERN
TERRITORY

Austrosaurus

Muttaburrasaurus

Minmi

QUEENSLAND

SOUTH
AUSTRALIA

Kakuru

NEW
SOUTH
WALES

Rhoetosaurus

Rapator

Qantassaurus

Timimus

Atlascopcosaurus

Leaellynasaura

VICTORIA

1

2

3

4

45

Glossary

ambush
To attack by surprise.

armoured dinosaur
A plant-eating dinosaur protected by tough scales or bony plates.

continent
One of Earth's seven huge areas of land. In the age of dinosaurs, the continents were in different positions than they are today.

crater
A deep hollow made by a volcano or by a meteor hitting Earth.

crest
A large flap on top of a dinosaur's head.

Cretaceous period
The last part of the age of dinosaurs, which ended suddenly when a meteor struck Earth.

dinosaur hunter
Someone who searches for dinosaur fossils and digs them up.

duck-billed dinosaur
A dinosaur with a mouth like a beak and no front teeth. Also known as a hadrosaur.

evolve
To change gradually over thousands or millions of years. As living things evolve, new types gradually appear, while older ones slowly become extinct, or die out.

extinct
No longer living anywhere on Earth. Dinosaurs are now extinct, in addition to many other giant reptiles.

fossil
Hard parts of an animal's body that have slowly changed to stone deep in the ground.

herd
A group of animals that live, feed and breed together.

horn
A hard body part with a sharp point, usually found on a dinosaur's head.

insect
A small animal with six legs such as a beetle or a bee. The first insects appeared long before the first dinosaurs.

Jurassic period
The middle part of the age of dinosaurs.

limb
A front or back arm or leg.

limestone
A type of layered rock that often contains fossils.

mammal
A warm-blooded animal that feeds its babies milk.

meteor
A piece of rock that has reached Earth from space.

naturalist
Someone who studies animals and plants.

nerves
Parts of the body that work like wiring, helping an animal feel and move.

Pangaea
A huge supercontinent that existed at the beginning of the age of dinosaurs.

predator
An animal that hunts other animals for its food.

prehistoric
Anything that lived in the distant past, long before human history began.

prey
An animal that is hunted and eaten by other animals.

quarry
A place where rock is dug up so that it can be used. Quarries are often good places for finding fossils.

reptile
A cold-blooded animal with scaly skin that usually breeds by laying eggs. Dinosaurs were the biggest reptiles that ever lived.

sauropod
A huge, long-necked dinosaur that fed on plants. The largest dinosaurs were all sauropods.

scales
Small, hard plates that cover a reptile's skin.

scavenging
Feeding on the remains of dead animals.

serrated
Having jagged edges.

trackway
A place where dinosaurs often walked, leaving fossilized footprints.

Triassic period
The first part of the age of dinosaurs.

46

Index

Each dinosaur name has a pronunciation guide in parentheses after its entry.

Photographic acknowledgments

The Publisher would like to thank the following for permission to reproduce their material. Every care has been taken to trace copyright holders. However, if there have been unintentional omissions or failure to trace copyright holders, we apologize and will, if informed, endeavour to make corrections in any future edition.

Pages: 5 Natural History Museum, London/Science Photo Library; 9 Wolfgang Kaehler/LightRocket via Getty; 13 Jim Amos/Science Photo Library; 15 Martin Leber/Shutterstock; 19 D. van Ravenswaay/Science Photo Library; 20 MAF/Alamy; 22 Dr Andrew Cuff; 24 Akkharat Jarusilawong/Shutterstock; 26 picturelibrary/Alamy; 27 University Corporation for Atmospheric Research/Science Photo Library; 29 Natural History Museum; 31 Didier Dutheil/Sygma via Getty Images; 33 Faviel_Raven/Shutterstock; 35 Arco Images GmbH/Alamy; 37 Natural History Museum; 39 Natural History Museum; 41 Louie Psihoyos/Corbis; 44 katclay/iStock